# THE CONSTRUCTION WORKER

*Amish Romance*

## HANNAH MILLER

Tica House
Publishing

Sweet Romance that Delights and Enchants!

# Personal Word from the Author

**To My Dear Readers,**

How exciting that you have chosen one of my books to read. Thank you! I am proud to now be part of the team of writers at Tica House Publishing who work joyfully to bring you stories of hope, faith, courage, and love.

Please feel free to contact me as I love to hear from my readers. I would like to personally invite you to sign up for updates and to become part of our **Exclusive Reader Club** —it's completely Free to join! Hope to see you there!

**With love,**

**Hannah Miller**

**VISIT HERE to Join our Reader's Club and to Receive Tica House Updates:**

https://amish.subscribemenow.com/

# Chapter One

Blue complimented her sisters, Hettie thought, as they donned the dresses she had made them. They were both, as she was, pale-skinned and freckled, with blue eyes a few shades darker than their *newehockers'* outfits. The dress on Jane was a little too big, though, especially about the waist and shoulders. Hettie would have to fix that. For her older sister, Claire, though, it fit perfectly. But then, she and Claire were about the same size, so it had been easier.

Jane grinned. "They're beautiful," she told her sister. "Thank you, Hettie. The wedding is going to be right nice."

Hettie smiled at the praise. "Yours will be better when I get it to fit," she said. "Now, hold still." She reached for the loose folds of fabric around Jane's waist and began slotting pins in place.

"I love weddings," Jane said with a sigh. "And yours will be perfect, Hettie. I mean, you and Henry, you're perfect for each other. It's going to be wonderful *gut*. This is the start of your whole future."

Hettie grinned at that. The thought was exciting. Nerve-wracking, too, but exciting, nonetheless. Of course, she had her doubts, but her mother had told her that was normal. This was a big step in her life. One of the biggest. Baptism in the church, marriage, and motherhood.

"You're too romantic, Jane," Claire said. She'd been quiet all day, but then, that wasn't so unusual for Claire. "Marriage is a duty and a sacred bond. It's not riding off in a buggy holding onto your fairy prince."

"Well, Henry does have a white horse," Hettie said. "And I'm sure we can find a crown for him."

Jane snickered, but Claire frowned.

"Anyway, I'm glad Henry isn't a fairy prince or anything like that. I much prefer the hard-working, down to earth sort."

"Really though, Hettie, you're so blessed. Finding a good man like Henry. I hope *I* can find a Henry one day."

"You will," Hettie told her younger sister. "You both will."

"Excuse me," Claire said, indignant. "But I've already got Samuel."

"Well *jah*, but has he asked to marry you?" Jane asked.

Hettie bit her lip at the death glare Claire shot Jane. Jane was, as usual, unknowingly aggravating Claire, and that spelled danger. Hettie didn't want a family falling-out so soon before her wedding.

"*Ach*, Jane," Hettie said, tightening the cloth around Jane's left shoulder and pinning it in place. "You know Samuel. He's always late in everything he does. He'll ask Claire soon enough. Not everything has to be on a schedule you know, especially love."

Claire sniffed. "Exactly," she said. "If Samuel wants to ask me, he'll do it in his own time."

"Well, he better not wait too long," Jane said. "Don't think I haven't seen Jonas Miller looking at you in church. If Samuel doesn't hurry up, Jonas will try and beat him to it, I bet."

Claire's cheeks reddened. "Nonsense," she muttered. "Besides, I wouldn't marry Jonas if he was the last man on earth."

Jane laughed. "*I* would. Have you *seen* his smile? Honestly, it's the like the whole world lights up when he smiles."

"There's more to a man than his smile," Hettie admonished. "And if you go thinking there isn't, you'll end up with the wrong man. Character is what's important. Whether they're dutiful, kind, loyal, patient, hardworking…"

"And be steady," Claire added.

"Well, I hardly think that's the most important thing, but all right, it helps."

"Well, we'll see," said Jane. "Besides, I haven't even joined church yet. I think I still have some time to decide what I want in a husband."

"You don't always get to decide," Claire said. "Sometimes you just fall for them."

Hettie frowned. Was Claire talking about Samuel? Was she saying she was in love with Samuel Raber? Claire was always so matter-of-fact, it was often hard to tell if she even *liked* Samuel. But it would be nice if she was in love, Hettie decided. Her sister deserved a bit of happiness.

She sent her sisters away, then, so she could get on with making the adjustments for Jane's dress. They had chores to do outdoors, anyway, and the three of them had spent so long talking, it would be a miracle if even half the work got done today.

Two weeks, that was all, she thought to herself as she stitched the blue fabric. Just two more weeks, and she would no longer be Hettie Mast, but Hettie Schwartz.

Henry was late, Hettie thought to herself, mildly annoyed. Henry was almost always punctual, so even a few minutes delay from him seemed like forever. She had already prepared lunch—a simple but delicious array of bread, cheese, cold meats, and sweet apple pie for dessert. He would be here soon enough, she told herself. Patience had always been a virtue she'd had to work exceedingly hard at. She decided to lay the table for the seven of them, hoping he wouldn't be too much later.

She was almost done when she heard the sound of his pony cart coming up the driveway, the wheels crunching over the gravel. Michael ran into the kitchen, a lightning bolt until she caught him and told him to calm down. Michael was almost eight now, the youngest of Hettie's four siblings, with the same fine blond hair and freckles as the rest of them.

"Henry's here," he said. "Does that mean it's mealtime?"

"Soon enough," Hettie told him. "Go and see if his horse needs anything."

Michael dashed out again, leaving Hettie to wonder if they would ever be able to sufficiently tame her youngest brother. She followed him out at a more sedate pace and smiled when she saw Henry heading toward her. Her heartbeat quickened. *Is this how you know you're in love?* she wondered.

"Sorry," Henry told her. "A tree's blown down over the road in that wind we had this morning. Took me and the entire Eicher family to move it to the side of the road."

"Oh, goodness," Hettie said. "Any earlier and it might have crushed you."

Henry shook his head. "Don't be silly. I'll bet it came down a *gut* few hours ago. It's a quiet road, which is why no one came across it before me."

"Well, I'm glad you're here now. We'll have a nice lunch, and most likely *Dat* will want to tell you all about the new barn we're starting tomorrow."

Henry groaned. "I'm sure I've heard everything about that barn ten times already."

Hettie giggled. "Well, can you bear eleven times? Maybe twelve?"

Henry sighed. "I suppose so."

Henry was quiet through lunch. He was often quiet and thoughtful, but Hettie thought he seemed distracted. Maybe he was as nervous about the wedding as she was.

After the meal, she decided to ask him about it.

"Are you all right?" she asked as they sat down on the porch together. The cold, windy morning had grown into a bright and sunny afternoon. Michael was busy chasing butterflies with Jane, who was more indulging him than actually playing herself.

Henry nodded. "Nothing to worry about," he said, but his smile seemed a little forced. "I just didn't sleep much last night."

"Are you nervous about the wedding?"

"Now why would you think that? We've been engaged for months now. I think I've adjusted to the idea." He chuckled.

"Well, *I'm* nervous, although perhaps I shouldn't tell you that. It's a big commitment after all. One I want to take, of course, and I'm so happy we're doing this—and that I'll get to spend the rest of my life with you, but it's a big step. It's not just about us, it's about being true under the eyes of *Gott*, and in a way, it's about stepping from childhood into adulthood fully."

Henry laughed at that. "Well, for you, maybe, but I'm already an adult, and have been for a while."

"*Jah*, all right. I know I'm younger, but... you know what I mean. Once we're married, we'll have *bopplis*, and that... well I'm excited for all of it, but it's still a lot, you know."

Henry glanced at her, briefly, and then cast his gaze off into the distance. "Hmm," he said. "I suppose you're right."

Trying to lighten the moment, Hettie teased, "Aren't I usually right?"

"*Jah*, my dear," he said, his gaze still distant. "Of course, you are."

# Chapter Two

It had been a few days since Hettie had heard from Henry. He had kissed her on the cheek as he'd said goodbye after the noon meal that day, and promised to see her very soon, but after that, nothing. He was, of course, always quite busy, and he hadn't specified a time or a date to come by, but with the wedding coming up, Hettie felt anxious to see him. She wanted to make sure he was fine, and to talk any last details through. Maybe she was being a little clingy, but she needed reassurance that everything was going right, that *this* was right.

She wanted to see his face, to hear his voice. Just his presence, knowing he was close by, had always been able to keep her grounded, to keep her anxieties from whirling her away.

So that morning, she decided to cycle to his place. Henry was the district's blacksmith, so she knew he would be in his workshop right then, probably working hard to finish all his outstanding work before the wedding. Henry always did work hard. It was one of the many things Hettie loved about him.

The morning was cool with the promise of another balmy afternoon, and Hettie enjoyed the feel of the temperate sun on her face as she rode.

She liked cycling into town—sometimes it felt as though she was moving between worlds. Her own world, with its horses and carts and plows and men tipping their hats to her as she passed, and the *Englisch* world, with its lights and cars and noise. Once, she had fancied herself living in the *Englisch* world, but that had been a fleeting, childish whimsy.

Now she found it strange that people could live like that, or the way they did in cities where everything was consume, consume, consume, with so little time or place for God. But she liked being here; this was a small town, and the people were friendly. The *Englisch* woman who ran the bakery waved to her as she passed, and a couple of young school children shouted greetings to her.

When she arrived at the blacksmith shop, she was surprised to find it closed. It wasn't a weekend or a holiday. Aside from the weekends, Henry was *always* here. Except today.

She headed around the back to see if the side door was open, but that too, was locked. How strange. Well, perhaps he was taking lunch, or he'd gone to work on site somewhere else.

She'd just have to come back tomorrow or take her brother and go to his house this evening to see if he was there. She had the fleeting thought that perhaps he had taken ill, but she dismissed it. Henry was never ill. In truth, she'd never known anyone so robust.

But that evening, he wasn't at home, nor was he at the shop the next morning.

Henry, it seemed, had vanished.

It took two days for Hettie to make up her mind. Fraught with worry and unable to concentrate on the baking preparations for the upcoming wedding, she decided she would have to hire a van and go visit Henry's hometown. His parents lived there, and they would know where he was. She knew things must be bad when Henry's best friend, Joe Farmer, came by to ask if she'd seen him. If Joe didn't know where Henry was, well, then no one here would.

But it was just possible that Henry's parents might. Perhaps he'd gone to visit them, seek out advice, or maybe one of them had been taken ill and he'd had to rush off. But then, why not tell her? Why not write? It had now been a week since she'd last seen him, and four days since she'd called by his shop to find him no longer there.

She told her parents she was going with Henry to visit his

family. His family's district was thirty miles away, so they weren't to worry if she was back late. Of course, they trusted her and accepted her words. That only made her feel worse about the deception. But she was so confused and worried that she couldn't bring herself to admit the truth. What would her parents think if they knew he'd vanished into thin air?

*Oh, Henry,* she thought. *What are you doing to me?*

She couldn't help the sinking feeling in her heart as she climbed into the hired van early that morning. She'd made arrangements with the driver to pick her up a bit down the road from her house. Otherwise, her parents would question why Henry hadn't been picked up first.

Having a plan and taking some action, gave her something to focus on. She would find out where Henry was, make sure he was okay, talk to him. Whatever was going on with him right now, she would find out soon enough.

Hettie arrived at Henry's parents' house less than an hour later. It was a small house, with a vast stretch of farmland behind it. Forty acres, he'd told her once, the last time they'd visited. She'd only been here once before, shortly after they'd become engaged. That had been a few months ago. She liked his parents; they seemed like good, honest people.

Henry's younger sister, not much older than Hettie, opened the door when she knocked. She seemed surprised to see Hettie there, but invited her inside anyway and made her some hot tea.

"What brings you here?" May asked as she took a seat across from her at the small kitchen table.

"Well, I-I'm looking for Henry..." Hettie's words came slowly. She already felt it—that Henry wasn't here after all. Otherwise May would have already gone to fetch him.

May bit her lip. "Henry... Do you mean he didn't talk to you?"

Hettie shook her head. "I haven't seen him for almost a week, and as you know, we're due to marry just a week from now."

"Oh." May frowned, leaving her tea untouched. "Well... I wish he'd talked to you. This isn't at all my place to tell you."

"Tell me what," Hettie said., her stomach tightening. "I just want to know if he's all right."

"Well, I haven't seen him. But Hettie, I've heard... *Ach*, I hate to say this. But I heard *Mamm* say that he's eloped with Catherine Raab. *Mamm* and *Dat* were talking about it two days ago, so I asked them for more details. They showed me the letter Henry left, telling them. I know that Catherine was Henry's first love, but she married someone else years back. She's been recently widowed, and well, in my opinion it's all a little unsavory, especially since he hadn't broken things off with you. We didn't know that. None of us did. We would have told you if we'd know. Truly, we would have. Actually, and maybe this is wrong of me, but I'm quite angry with him for this. It ain't right."

Nausea roared through Hettie. She clung to the edge of the table as her whole world tilted sideways. Had she heard May correctly? No. No. No. Surely not. May must have gotten it wrong.

But was there really some woman Hettie had neither met nor heard of, whom Henry still loved? Had he really left her for this other woman? Had he really been such a coward that he hadn't even said *anything* to her? That he'd let her continue to make wedding plans when the whole time he'd had no intention of coming back or marrying her at all?

No. It *couldn't be*. But looking at the expression of pity on May's face forced the reality of it.

Hettie felt... numb. She shook her head and tried to keep breathing. She couldn't make sense of it. It was too much. Tears burned behind her eyes, and she blinked them back, not wanting to show May how upset she was. Instead, she forced herself to nod—forced herself to take a sip of the scalding tea.

"I ... I understand," she said. "Thank you for being honest with me, May. If that's the case, then... Well, Henry isn't quite the man I thought he was."

"*Nee*," May agreed. "I'm not sure he is. *Ach*, I'm so sorry Hettie. Truly, I am."

"I think," Hettie said, pushing back her chair and standing, "that I should take my leave."

May nodded, her face nearly crumpling in tears. "I'm sorry," she said again. "Do you need a ride somewhere? *Mamm* and *Dat* have taken the buggy, but the pony cart is still here."

Hettie shook her head. Walking would do her some good. Her driver had told her he would be returning to Greendale Grove that afternoon. She knew, roughly, the way to town from her last visit here, and it wasn't so far to walk, perhaps just an hour away. She would find a phone shanty and make arrangements to be picked up in town instead of at Henry's family farm.

She started off walking, her mind numb, her feet carrying her as if independently. She stared straight ahead, only pausing when she had to make sure she was still going the right direction. She found a phone shanty and made her call. She arrived in town before noon and sat on a park bench and waited for her van to show up. When it finally did, she crawled into the backseat and after mumbling a greeting to the drive, didn't say a word all the way home.

# Chapter Three

"That was a short trip," Claire said, frowning as Hettie entered the house. Claire was in the sitting room, darning. She seemed to be the only one inside. "How is Henry?"

Hettie forced a smile. "Oh, Henry? He's doing just fine. His mother, though, she's very sick..."

*Where was this lie coming from?* she wondered even as it spilled out of her mouth. What was she doing?

"He has to stay there to take care of her and help on the farm. You know, he only has the one sister, and she's a little frail herself..." That also was not true, and Hettie hated herself not just for the lie but for the elaboration of it. "We've decided to postpone the wedding."

"*Ach, nee,*" Claire said, setting aside her darning. "Hettie, I'm so sorry."

Hettie shook her head. She would *not* cry. "*Nee,* it's the right thing to do. Family must come first. And when his mother is well again, we'll reset the date. I imagine we'll still be married by the end of the year."

"What a shame though," Claire said. "And being so close to the day as well. Still, I suppose it can't be helped."

"*Nee,*" Hettie said stiffly. "It can't be helped."

"Have you told *Mamm* yet?"

Hettie twisted her hands together and shook her head. "Not yet. I'll tell everyone over dinner. Right now, I need to rest."

Claire nodded. "Of course. We weren't expecting you back until later, so Jane and I have done most of your chores already anyway."

"Thank you," Hettie said, forcing another smile. "That's appreciated."

She left her sister to finish her darning and took the stairs up to the room the two of them shared. She was glad to be alone right now. She needed to think. She had lied to her sister, and she already knew she would continue that lie. She would tell it again to the rest of her family, and they would tell it to their friends. She knew she should tell the truth; she knew it down to her toes, but she couldn't do it. Not yet. It was too hurtful, too humiliating.

How could Henry *have done this* to her?

Today would have been her wedding day, the day when she had planned to commit to Henry for the rest of her life, the day she was to have become Mrs. Schwartz. Hettie had barely slept the night before, or the night before that, or really for the past week since she'd learned of Henry's deception.

Everyone was tiptoeing around her. Even though she hadn't told them the truth, they were still sorry for her. They kept asking how Henry was, how his mother was doing. And Hettie just kept lying. She knew it was wrong, but the other option, to tell the truth ... was just too difficult. Everyone would know her shame. She couldn't face it right now.

Hettie had gotten up early that morning, well before dawn, to find the cows had pulled down part of a fence. As the sun rose, she headed toward it with a roll of wire and a bag of tools. She couldn't fix what had happened with Henry; she couldn't mend her plans for the wedding or the rest of her life, but she could mend this fence. Even if her father would see to it later, she wanted to do it.

She was almost done when the rage took hold. This was supposed to be her wedding day. How *dare* Henry do this to her? How could he just leave without so much as a word? She swung the hammer too hard, and the nail split the post with a *crack*. She flung the hammer to the ground, fighting back the urge to scream.

When she returned to the house, the fence crudely mended but in poor shape, she was composed again. No one would see the pain she was carrying. They *couldn't* know. She avoided her family, as she had been more or less avoiding them all week, trying to keep herself busy, focused, and alone. She went to the room she shared with Claire, thankful it was empty, and prayed.

She couldn't hear any answer, but it made her feel a little better. No matter how bad things were, *Gott* was always there, listening. *He* knew the truth of it all, and, she hoped, he understood. She would have to confess sometime, she knew. But not yet. Not quite yet...

She sat for a while, thinking. She needed something else in her life. Something to take her mind off things. A change of direction. Hadn't she seen an ad while she was running errands in town a couple of days ago? The local construction firm was wanting to hire a cleaner. It wasn't something she'd considered before, but now... Well, maybe now what she needed was a little independence and a new direction.

Hettie knew some girls who had taken jobs in the town, who had talked about the sense of freedom it gave them, who told interesting little stories about their day-to-day working lives.

And maybe, if Hettie were working, it would give people something to ask about other than Henry Schwartz and their 'delayed' wedding.

*Jah,* she thought. *It is a good idea.*

She would have to speak to her parents about it, of course, but she thought they could manage without her being on the farm for a few days a week. After all, if she *had* married Henry, she would have gone to live with him and wouldn't be there at all. Her folks were reasonable people. She was sure they'd agree. This position, she was sure now, was exactly what she needed.

Hettie began work the following week. Although the company, Wright Construction, was owned by an *Englisch* man, there were several Amish men who worked there, and after speaking to some of them, Hettie's parents had allowed her to interview for the job. And the very next day, she had been told she could start work. Her shifts were longer than she'd imagined, from 11am until 6pm. She hadn't thought a small company would need so much cleaning done, but the building was large, and there was sweeping of the workshop floor, cleaning down the benches, cleaning the staff bathrooms and break room, and making sure everything was tidy again for the next morning.

Hettie kept her head down at work, focusing on learning her

new routine and getting her job done. And she did her tasks with great care. She meant to make the company pleased.

It wasn't until her third day that she began to remember the names of the other workers. They were a friendly bunch, always saying hello and asking after her family. She liked that. It was like a little mini-community. Thursday night, she decided to bake cupcakes for the office, and she left them in the staff room with a note for people to help themselves.

"You," one *Englisch* man told her, "are the best cleaner we've had. Myrtle was good, but she never brought us cupcakes."

Hettie blushed at that, trying to stamp down the little well of pride that came with pleasing people.

"Smart idea that," another man told her. Hettie knew him from church. His name was Amos Wengerd, and she knew he lived with his sister and his *aenti* on a small property just a few miles away from Hettie's family home. She had seen him around occasionally, although they had never really spoken. He was a few years older than she, and his family had moved to Greendale Grove from Pennsylvania about six years back when Amos was already finished with school. Hettie knew his younger sister Alice a little better. They had gone to school together but had never really become close friends.

"Easy way to get people to like you," he continued.

"I didn't do it to be liked," Hettie told him defensively. "I did it because you all work so hard, and I thought you deserved a treat."

Amos smiled. His smile was a little crooked, and Hettie noticed one of his teeth was chipped. "What I meant to say was 'thank you'. It's appreciated."

Hettie returned his smile and went back to cleaning down the counters.

It wasn't a cure, this job, but it did take her mind off her situation, just a little. She had something to focus on now, at least for a good portion of the day. But that didn't mean Hettie didn't occasionally find herself drifting into thoughts of Henry while she was mopping the floors, nor did it stop her from every morning wondering what was so wrong with her that he would leave like that. More than once, she teared up while she was in the bathroom, but she was more able to push those thoughts and feelings to the side for the sake of the work.

# Chapter Four

One evening, Hettie headed into the warehouse to give the floor one last sweep and to empty the bins before she went home. She found Amos still there, almost an hour after everyone else had finished for the day. He was measuring boards, marking the places on them he needed to cut. Hettie didn't say anything to him, not wanting to interrupt —he seemed so focused on his work. Instead, she took the bins, replaced the liners, and headed out the back to dump them.

He glanced up at her as she came back in. "Oh," he said, "Do you need to lock up?"

Hettie shook her head. "Mr. Wright locks up at eight, so don't worry. There's no need to stop on my account."

Amos grinned. "Well, it's about time I finished this up, I

suppose. I just can't help myself sometimes. I get into the work, and time just slips away from me."

Hettie couldn't help but admire his work ethic. Clearly, he valued his labor, and wasn't someone to watch the clock, only thinking about when he could get away. That, Hettie thought, was the way it should be.

"Well," she said, feeling a little awkward all of a sudden, "you have a good night, Mr. Wengerd."

Amos nodded. "You too, Miss Mast."

Although he'd meant it cheerfully and kindly, his words sank like a knife between her ribs. She turned away from him and headed out of the building with her chin up, but her eyes burning. *Miss Mast.* Not Mrs. Schwartz. She would *never* be Mrs. Schwartz. She would most likely never be Mrs. Anything.

She tried to push back the cascade of bitterness that threatened to engulf her as she cycled back to the homestead. She tried to focus on the slight burn in her legs as she pedaled faster and faster, the cool evening wind biting her face and hands as she rushed by the dark hedgerows alongside her. All her hopes had been crushed. Her future, gone. She was unwanted, just 'Miss Mast' for the rest of her days.

She didn't go into the house right away, but instead sat quietly on the porch, looking out at the black, shadowy world around her.

"What are you doing out here?" Jane asked, closing the front door behind her. "There's dinner left for you. Stew. I made it. It's still in a pot on the stove."

"Thank you," Hettie said, "But I'm not so hungry. Perhaps later."

Jane took a seat beside her. She was getting tall now, Hettie realized.

"You must be missing Henry terribly."

Hettie winced. "Yes," she said stiffly.

"He doesn't write much, does he?"

"*Nee.* He's very busy with his mother." The lie twisted and barbed inside her, cutting deep.

"He will," Jane promised. "And I'm sure his *mamm* will be well soon. You and Henry will be together again. You're perfect for each other."

Hettie was glad Jane couldn't see her face in the dark. "Oh *jah,* I'm sure we will be together soon," she said. She too, had thought she and Henry perfect for one another. Clearly, Henry had not thought so. How had she missed that? Had she really been so blind? How could she not have known that he didn't love her?

And *why* had he pretended he did?

Jane patted her on the shoulder, then stood. "Food's there

when you want it," she said, and headed back inside, leaving Hettie alone once more.

When Hettie arrived at work the next day, most of the men were out on a job, but Amos was there, his back to her as he worked with the saw, cutting out the panels he had been measuring the previous evening. She left him to it and began with the most important task—cleaning the toilets and washing the floors. She then vacuumed Mr. Wright's office and dusted everything down in the reception room where clients came in. She cleaned the windows and the tiles, jobs that were to be done every other day, but that she hadn't done the day before.

After the men had eaten their lunch, she cleaned the staff room, neatened the cushions on the small couch, and emptied the bins. It wasn't until halfway through her day, that she realized she had not thought about Henry even once. She smiled to herself, perhaps a bit thin-lipped, but still... This was good. It was how it should be. She owed that man nothing, and he needn't be taking up any more time in her head, she decided. She had to move on with her life.

Of course, there was the matter of the lies she had told everyone, but couldn't she worry about that later? She was only beginning to feel better. If she told the truth now, the pitying looks would start all over again.

She began to hum to herself a little as she worked, chasing away any lingering negative thoughts and keeping only the positive. Today had been a good day for her, and she planned to keep it that way.

"You seem in a *gut* mood," Amos commented as he entered the staff room, his tea mug in one hand.

"And why shouldn't I be?" she asked with a smile.

"Of course, you *should* be, I just haven't seen you in one since you started here. Truth be told, I've been a bit concerned about you."

Hettie set down the rag she'd been cleaning the microwave with and set her hands upon her hips as if she were vexed. "You should mind your own business about my moods," she said lightly, only teasing.

Amos chuckled, a throaty sort of sound, with merriment in his dark eyes. "You're quite right, I suppose," he told her. "I should keep my nose out."

"*Ach,* I'm only kidding," she told him and went back to her cleaning.

"Glad to hear it," he said, as he set the kettle on the two-burner hotplate to boil for his tea. "How are you finding it here? You seem in a *gut* routine now."

"Oh, I like it well enough," Hettie said. "Keeps me busy. And

I suppose you lot aren't terrible. Although someone does keep spilling soup all over this contraption."

"Well, don't look at me. I always bring sandwiches. No mess, no fuss."

"Very sensible," Hettie agreed, working at a stubborn stain on the inside of the door.

"So will you be working here until your Henry comes back?"

Hettie stiffened. So, he knew about her and Henry, too? "*Jah*, I suppose so," she said.

Amos sighed. "Bit of bad luck there. How's his mother doing?"

"No better," Hettie told him, "but thankfully, no worse either. We're hopeful she'll recover soon though."

Amos nodded, and poured his tea. "Would you like a cup?"

Hettie looked at him, and then back at the stain she was working on. Well, just one cup couldn't hurt, and she hadn't had a break yet.

He fetched her a clean mug and poured her some hot water and plopped in a teabag. It was a fragrant tea that smelled more of lavender than anything else.

"You went to school with my sister, *ain't so?*" Amos asked, taking a sip of his tea. Amos had only the one sister, as well as one older brother who had stayed in Pennsylvania with his wife and young child when the rest of the family had moved to Indiana. It was strange how much you could know about a person despite having never really met them properly. But then of course when the Wengerds had first moved to town, everyone had been talking about them, and Hettie couldn't help but remember some of it.

She nodded and sipped her own tea. It was a little strong for her liking, and she fought the urge to sneeze. Give her a simple lemon tea any day, or the apple and cinnamon blend her mother sometimes made.

"Alice? *Jah,* I did. But we didn't know each other very well. She was a little older, and had other friends, so we only spoke occasionally. She seemed nice, though. Smart, too."

Amos chuckled. "*Jah,* she always was the bright one in the family."

"I think my little brother's the smart one in ours. He's eight, and already knows more than me. He's really into wildlife facts at the moment. I think he knows the name of every species of bird that ever graces our yard."

"Ah, *jah.* I think I've seen him by the river a few times, watching the waders."

Hettie nodded. "It's one of his favorite places."

"It's a *gut* spot," Amos agreed. He drained the last of his tea and stood. "Well, back to work, I suppose."

Hettie took his mug along with hers to the sink, telling him she'd wash up for the both of them, since he'd made the tea. He thanked her and headed back into the workshop.

He was still there when Hettie was doing her end-of-day clean, and once again, she left him to his work, wondering if it might be midnight by the time he was done.

# Chapter Five

Over the next weeks, Hettie began to feel a little better. Her heart was still bruised, but she felt like it might be beginning to finally heal. What was done was done, she decided, and there was little point dwelling on it. She prayed daily for guidance, for strength, and for the ability to forgive. But forgiveness was not something she could quite manage just yet. She was still angry and confused at times. But much less so than she had been before.

Sunday, her family attended preaching service, *Dat* driving them all in the buggy. Previously, Hettie had felt as though everyone was watching her. She'd had to endure well-meaning sympathies and people asking how Henry was doing. She'd lied to all of them. But this week, no one asked her how she was, or how Henry was doing. It was old news. And for that, she was grateful.

It was curious, though, that Henry hadn't yet come back to his blacksmith shop, and the district had to continue going to the neighboring town for service. Hettie had heard some talk about finding a temporary replacement until Henry could return. Folks had stopped asking her for the date of his return, as she couldn't tell them. Secretly, she hoped he would be gone a long, long time—if not forever.

That service, she sat with her sisters beside her, and breathed in every word the bishop spoke. He talked about sacrifice, patience, and forgiveness. Life was a struggle, he told them, a test. That made a lot of sense to Hettie. Maybe *Gott* was testing her. Wrapped up in herself, she hadn't thought of that, or that He might have some sort of plan for her. Instead, she'd been selfish, self-pitying, and whatever test He had designed for, she had likely failed with her lies.

*I must do better*, she thought. *I must try to prove myself worthy.*

She had to confess. Not just reshape the lie to distract everyone. She had to tell the truth, all of it. Right now, though, was not the time. She just hoped she would recognize the 'right time' when it came.

Hettie sipped her glass of water, her copy of *Robinson Crusoe* open in her lap. It was warm today, and she'd been working up a sweat. She hadn't planned to take more than a five-minute break—there was so much to be done—but Mr. Wright had insisted; all his staff were to take at *least* half an hour's break, even if they worked less than eight hours a day.

A few of the men were on break the same time she was. There were usually a few who stayed to complete tasks in the workshop, while the rest were out on jobs at building sites and homes. The company employed forty workers in total. For Greendale Grove, it was a big business. Hettie generally kept to herself, engaging in light conversation only occasionally. She hadn't felt much in the mood to socialize over the past few weeks, instead deciding to focus on her work.

"Good book," Amos said, peering at the cover. "Although of course Man Friday is the real hero of the novel."

"I couldn't agree more," Hettie said, putting the book down open on the table and reaching for her water. "I've read this one three times now."

Amos chuckled. "I'm afraid I've only read it the once. I never seem to find much time for reading."

"That's because you're always so busy working here," Hettie told him.

"True," he said. "I could make time if I wanted, but, well..."

"Reading is a luxury, not a priority, I suppose. I don't often have the time myself, and when I do read, it's usually the Bible. But I just felt like some good old-fashioned adventure today."

"Sensible," he said. "And sensible to carry it with you, in case you have time. Anyway, I should let you get back to it. Enjoy."

Hettie shot him a tentative smile. It was nice to have friends, she thought, and yes, she believed she and Amos Wengerd were becoming just that.

She managed to read a couple more pages before deciding her break was over—five minutes earlier than mandated, but she had work to do after all. She spent the rest of the day sweeping and mopping and dusting, and her back ached a little by the end of the day. She hadn't slept well the night before, too much tossing and turning. Claire had shouted at her once to *Just go to sleep,* because the bed frame creaked every time Hettie turned. She would have to try and fix that when she got home so as not to disturb her again.

Amos was, as usual, still there at the end of the day, stacking away bags of concrete that had come in on a late delivery.

"I'm off now," she told him. She always told him when she was going if he was still there—just so he knew he was now alone in the building, aside from Mr. Wright.

Amos set down the concrete mix and turned to look at her. His expression was... Hettie couldn't quite read it. Curious, maybe? Still warm, but something unknown underneath. She turned to go.

"Have a *gut* night," he told her. "See you tomorrow."

Hettie shot him a smile over her shoulder. "*Jah*, see you tomorrow," she promised.

As she cycled home, she thought about her lies—about the lie that Amos, along with everyone else, believed. That she was still betrothed, that her wedding was only postponed, that Henry hadn't left her for a woman Hettie had never even met.

What would Amos think of her if he knew? Why had she done this? She had wanted to avoid humiliation and shame, but she had only hurt herself further by lying, for now when she confessed, the humiliation and shame would be so much greater than it would have been if she'd just told the truth in the first place.

The next day, Hettie didn't see Amos. He was out on a site on the other side of town. Work always felt a little less... well, just a little different somehow, when Amos wasn't there. But she pushed that feeling to one side and carried on with her work. There wasn't quite so much to do today, and she welcome it when Mr. Wright told her she could probably leave early that evening if she wanted. There were chores to be done at home, and she still hadn't gotten around to fixing her bed frame (although she *had* slept a little better last night and hadn't woken Claire up once).

She was busy cleaning the small reception area when Freya, who worked the desk, returned from her break, a mug of coffee in her hands. She wore an unusually serious expression. "Have you heard the news?" she asked.

Hettie shook her head. She'd barely spoken to anyone all day.

"You know Amos Wengerd, right? One of our workers? Well, he had a fall on site this morning. He was up on some scaffolding at those new houses out at Lily River."

Hettie almost dropped her broom but caught it and clutched the handle tightly. "Is he badly hurt?" she managed to ask, trying to stay calm.

"He's in the hospital. Hit his head apparently, and has some broken bones. Mr. Wright is on his way over to see him now."

"Is anyone with him?"

"Lucas went with him in the ambulance."

Lucas was the site supervisor. It was good of him to go with Amos, to make sure he got to the hospital safely. And it was good of Mr. Wright to go and check on him, too. But it didn't make Hettie feel any better. She wished *she* were there. She would make sure Amos was looked after properly.

*Don't be so silly,* she told herself. That wasn't her job. She wasn't family, was barely even a friend. Still, she wanted to be there. She wanted to see for herself that he was okay. She had to sternly remind herself that rushing to his side now wouldn't be appropriate.

"Has anyone gone to tell his family?" Hettie asked.

"Not yet. I said I'd call, but... no phones I guess." Freya gave a slight shrug and bit her lip. "But Mr. Wright said he'd go over after he's been to the hospital."

Amos didn't have much family left in town, Hettie knew. His mother had passed away a few years back, his father last fall. There was only his sister and his elderly *aenti* now. But they would take good care of him.

*So, you don't need to worry,* she told herself firmly. But it didn't help any. She would keep on fretting about him until she actually saw him herself.

Freya slumped into her office chair. "What a day," she groaned. She stretched a little and tugged at her suit jacket to straighten it. "But he'll be all right, I'm sure," she said, as if making a conscious effort at optimism. "I'll organize a card and flowers for him. You'll sign it, won't you?"

"Of course," Hettie told her. "It'll do him some *gut* I imagine, to know we're all thinking of him."

Freya smiled. "Exactly," she said. "I'll sort something out this afternoon then."

Hettie loved her a little for that. She'd never spoken with Freya much before now, but she could see the young woman had a good heart.

She tried to focus on her work, then, but her thoughts kept drifting to Amos. *Gott, please let him be all right.*

# Chapter Six

It had been a couple of days since Mr. Wright had announced that Amos had been released from hospital. Amos had stayed a few days for a concussion and then surgery on his leg. He wouldn't be back at work for a while, Mr. Wright told them.

Hettie couldn't help but wonder how Amos would cope with being bed-ridden. Amos was a man who liked to keep busy, who liked to be useful. Hettie couldn't imagine him enjoying just lying there and resting. No, most likely he'd be grumbling at his *aenti* and his sister and trying to get up when he shouldn't.

Hettie decided then that she had to visit. It would take his mind off things, give him something to occupy a moment with. And she would take him some baked goods and perhaps a book, so he wouldn't be too bored. She couldn't go alone, of course. One of her sisters would have to come with her.

"Hettie, I can't," Claire told her, frowning. "I'm busy. I've got so many chores to do here, and I'm supposed to be meeting Samuel for dinner at his parent's house. This is a big moment for us, you know? We've never done this before. So, I'm sorry, but I really can't."

Hettie sighed, and turned to her younger sister. Jane's answer was much more satisfactory.

"Of course," Jane said. "The poor man has had quite an ordeal. It's our Christian duty to go and cheer him up. Oh, maybe we could sing to him? Which hymn do you think he would like best?"

Singing was perhaps a bit much, Hettie thought, and although Jane's voice wasn't bad, her own would likely leave poor Amos in worse shape than he was in to begin with. "I think perhaps baking and *gut* conversation will be enough, Jane. We don't want to overwhelm him. He's had a concussion, after all."

Jane nodded seriously. "*Jah,* you're right. I didn't think of that. He might still have a headache. We shall have to be very quiet."

They spent the morning baking. Just a few things, an apple pie made with the last of the winter preserves from the basement, a loaf of raisin bread, and some savory rolls. Hettie didn't want to go *too* overboard, so she made herself stop there. They packed the things into a basket, along with Hettie's copy of *Wind in the Willows* to provide Amos some entertainment, and they set off.

They walked. The Wengerd family home wasn't far from their own, just a little more than two or three miles down a couple of the more scenic country lanes, past the Millers' apple orchard and the stream that connected to the river in town. Spring was in full bloom now, and blossoms were starting to fall from many of the trees, lining the paths with white petals. The day was warm, but with a cool breeze, and Hettie felt content.

Set far back from the road, the Wengerd house was tall and white with a high, sloping roof. There were blossoming cherry trees lining the left-hand path and chickens roaming free in the grass. It was a small block of land, with few animals—only the chickens and a couple of dairy cows as far as Hettie could see. She knew Amos's *aenti* was a seamstress, and his sister worked in the fabric shop in town.

It was Amos's sister, Alice, who answered the door. She seemed surprised to see them, but then realization dawned on her face. "You're here to see Amos?"

"*Jah,* we've brought him over a few things."

Alice nodded. "Thank you, that's very kind. I didn't realize you knew each other, though?"

"We work together," Hettie told her. "I do the cleaning at

Wright Construction. Since I live so close, I told the others I'd check in. Everyone sends their sympathies."

Alice nodded. "They've been very *gut*. Mr. Wright especially. I think he feels guilty, but it's not his fault. Accidents happen."

"How is Amos?" Hettie asked. "Is he up to visitors?"

"He's on the mend," Alice promised. "But he won't be up and about for a few weeks at least. Months, if I had my way. He needs to heal. You know, his right leg was fractured in three places, and his hip was bruised. They had to put pins in his leg to hold it together."

Hettie winced; it sounded painful. She didn't like to think of Amos being in pain.

"But mostly he's just annoyed he has to lie here and do nothing. I think he could use the rest if I'm being totally honest. It's *Gott's* way of telling him to slow down and take care of himself. He's upstairs. I'll just go up and check if he's awake."

She left them in the ample kitchen while she went to check on him. There was a pan of elderberries in the sink and a pot on the stove ready to cook them in. The room was clean and tidy, much like the yard outside. The house was a bit on the small side, but it was well kept.

Alice gestured for them to come up, and Hettie took the lead with Jane behind her. She entered the room to see Amos sitting up in his bed, propped up by several pillows. His dark hair was a little wild, and he looked much too pale for Hettie's liking. He was wearing a loose shirt, undone at the wrists, and he looked just as surprised to see her as Alice had been.

"Well, this a nice surprise," he said stiffly, almost as though it was anything but.

Hettie didn't let his tone get to her. He was likely still in pain. She set the basket down on the bed beside him.

"This is my sister, Jane," Hettie said, gesturing to Jane, who was suddenly quiet, as she often was around people she didn't know well. "We've brought you a few things," she said. "Of course, to share with your wonderful family."

Amos worked to smile. "I wasn't expecting you. I, well, I wish I was up."

"Of course," Hettie said. "I'm sure you'll be up in no time."

Amos sighed and pushed himself up to sit a little straighter. He winced, and Hettie felt for him.

"Thank you," he said, glancing into the basket. "This is very kind of you, but you really shouldn't have. I don't need to be fussed over."

"I'm not fussing," Hettie said sternly. "I'm letting you know people are wishing you well, and I thought a brief visit might help stop you from going stir crazy over here. I know you like to stay busy."

"It's only been a few days, and I already feel like I'm going crazy," Amos admitted. "I don't think I can stand weeks of this. I'm afraid patience is a virtue I'm a bit lacking in."

Hettie smiled, having suspected as much. "Just take it one day at a time," she told him. "I'll pray for a quick recovery for you. Although that *might* be a slightly selfish prayer. I miss your conversation at work."

Amos chuckled. "You need to make some new friends there. Stop keeping your head down so much of the time."

"With time," she told him. "But I'm finally starting to settle in. Baking for everyone helps, of course."

"*Gut*," Amos said, and then he yawned. "Sorry. I don't know why I'm so tired. It's not like I've been doing very much."

"You're recovering," Hettie told him. "You're bound to be tired."

Amos frowned. "If you say so," he said. "Thank you again for the things. And Jane, it was nice to meet you."

Jane smiled. Hettie nodded, knowing well enough that this was her cue to leave. She bid him a good day and turned to go, ushering Jane out of the door.

"He seemed..." Jane said, once were back outside and on their way home. "Grumpy."

Hettie didn't disagree, but then he was in pain. Their conversations had always been short, anyway. Still, he had seemed almost displeased to see them in the beginning.

Perhaps he hadn't liked her to see him like that—she knew Amos had a certain amount of pride in him. Or perhaps, he'd thought it was inappropriate for her to be visiting, since she was, after all, and as far as he or anyone else knew, engaged. She hoped that wasn't the case. She didn't want Amos to think badly of her.

But he'd softened there at the end, she thought. Maybe he was just trying to be nice, but she thought that perhaps he *had* been glad of her company, at least a little.

She certainly hoped so, anyway.

She faltered. Was she just a little ... *fond* of Amos Wengerd? Surely not. It was far too soon after Henry for those sorts of feelings. No, she was confusing her sympathies and her concern for him as a friend, that was all.

That *had* to be all.

# Chapter Seven

Hettie didn't visit Amos again. She couldn't be sure he'd appreciate it, and she didn't want anyone, least of all Amos, to get the wrong idea about her intentions.

She couldn't help but think about him though, and she prayed for his recovery and his patience with it, every day. Jane often asked about him too, now, and said she would keep him in her prayers. That was nice of her, Hettie thought. Jane would certainly grow into a good, kind woman. She just hoped that Jane would have more luck with men than she herself had.

It was another three weeks before Amos was back at work. Hettie couldn't believe her eyes when she saw him in the workshop, a pair of crutches leaning against his workbench. What on earth was he thinking? He should still be at home recovering.

"I couldn't stand it," Amos told her, when she asked, a little more politely, why he was here. "I need to be useful, and Mr. Wright has some tasks I can do right here, so I don't really need to use my legs all that much."

Hettie frowned at him.

"You disapprove," he said, matter-of-factly. "Well, don't worry, I'm not overdoing it. I'll be heading home at four. I'm under strict orders, apparently."

"I'm glad to hear it," Hettie said.

"It was nice of you to visit that day," Amos told her, then. "Sorry if I was grouchy. If I'm honest, I was a bit surprised to see you."

"Well, we were all wondering how you were doing, and I thought you might be getting rather bored being stuck in bed."

"Oh, trust me, I was."

"You'll be glad to know not much has changed here in your absence. Except Freya from reception and Paul who does the accounting are apparently engaged."

Amos's eyebrows raised. "*Ach*, really? *Gut* for them. They're both very nice people."

"Yes, they are rather," Hettie agreed.

"And what about you?" Amos asked. "How's Henry doing? Have you set a new date for the wedding yet?"

Hettie's heart twisted. Her parents had recently been asking the same thing. It had been over a month now since Henry's departure, and Hettie still hadn't confessed the truth. "His mother is still quite ill, but on the mend. We won't set a new date until she's well again. You know how things go. It could be days, weeks, or months before she's fully recovered. Anyway, you're busy, I'd best let you get on with things. And I have bins to empty."

She scuttled away, leaving Amos to his work. She didn't want to talk about Henry. She wanted to forget him entirely, but of course, how could she, given that everyone thought they were still to be married?

It was beyond time, she thought. She'd put it off far too long.

Hettie didn't sleep well that night. She tossed and stewed, her mind turning over and over the ramifications of her lies. Would her parents disown her? They'd be angry, certainly. Embarrassed and ashamed to have a daughter who could lie to them so easily. Maybe they'd be regretful that she hadn't been good enough for Henry Schwartz, that he'd chosen another woman over her. They thought she was a good girl, a responsible young woman who did her chores and said her prayers, who was kind and worked hard, but none of that had been enough. They, and everyone else, would know that there was something lacking in her. Like Henry, they would know was not enough.

She finally fell asleep in the early hours of the morning, with the sky lightening from black to bruised. She arose later than usual, when the sun was up in the sky. Jane was sitting on the end of her bed, her hand on Hettie's leg, shaking her awake.

Hettie sat bolt upright. "*Ach, nee.* Am I late for work?"

Jane shook her head, "*Nee* but... Hettie, is it true?"

Hettie frowned. She still felt half asleep. "Is what true?"

"Henry... Claire says she saw him in town yesterday. He came back yesterday afternoon apparently. With *his new wife.*"

Hettie froze. Henry was *back*? *Why*? Had she been such a fool as to assume he would stay gone? That would have been the decent thing for him to. But of course, Henry was really not that decent.

Tears burned in Hettie's eyes, and she covered her gaping mouth with her hand. She hadn't wanted them to find out like this.

"It *is* true, then," Jane said. "Why, Hettie? Did you know? And if you did, why would you lie to us?"

"I-I'm sorry," Hettie said, tears sliding down her cheeks now. "I felt like such a fool. And you... You all would think there's something wrong with me."

Jane shook her head. "We would never think that. But you shouldn't have lied to us, Hettie."

"Are *Mamm* and *Dat* very angry?"

"I think they're a bit confused. They want to talk with you. Now."

Reluctantly, Hettie nodded. Jane left her, and she got dressed, slowly. She didn't want to go downstairs, into the kitchen where she knew they'd be waiting at the table, her mother's hands clasped tightly together and her father thin-lipped and frowning. They wouldn't understand, she knew. Jane didn't understand, not really... And Jane was the most forgiving of them all. The look on her face had been one of raw disappointment, like her big sister had really let her down.

Hettie wiped the tears from her eyes, tied her apron securely about her waist, and headed downstairs to face them.

Hettie sat at the kitchen table, her hands twisted together in her lap, her teeth worrying her lower lip. Her parents sat in front of her, side-by-side, a united front. She couldn't meet their eyes, couldn't look at them. She was too ashamed.

"*Why*, Hettie? Why wouldn't you just tell us the truth?" her mother asked, echoing Jane's sentiments from earlier.

"You've lied. Over and over again. And *Henry*. I can't *believe* he's done this," her father muttered.

"He seemed like such a nice man," her mother said. "Truth be told, I don't know what to make of it all."

They were sorry for her, both of them, angry with Henry for jilting her, disappointed that someone they had approved of, had hurt her. And they were disappointed with her, for lying and for not having the strength of character to hold her head high and tell the truth.

"No one would have blamed you," her mother said forcefully. "You'd done nothing wrong. But now, with these lies... *Ach*, I don't know what I'm going to tell people."

Her father turned to face his wife. "You can tell nothing," he said sharply.

Hettie wanted to melt into the floor, to shrink away until she disappeared. This was what she'd been avoiding the whole time—this pity and disappointment. But by lying, she'd only exacerbated it, because now, she realized, she'd made herself look weak and lacking in character. She had been weak, too. There was no getting around it.

She couldn't let them down like this again, couldn't let herself down again, *ever*. Honesty had always been important to her, and she had given it up all too quickly.

"I'm sorry," she said, her voice sounding much stronger than she felt. "I know, I've let you all down. I can only pray to be better and to make amends. I didn't want to break your trust, but ... I know I have. I'll earn it back again. I will. I promise. As for Henry... I'm glad now, that I didn't marry him. He isn't the man I thought he was. I should have just admitted that. But... I-I was afraid."

Her mother stood, then, came around the table to wrap her arms around her daughter. Hettie leaned into her mother's embrace. Despite the mess and humiliation she had caused, she felt, surprisingly, almost relieved.

Hettie arrived to work five minutes late that morning. Her father had insisted on driving her. They spoke little, although he cleared his throat a few times, as though he was about to say something. But they had already said everything there was to say. Both her parents were still disappointed and angry. And confused. They'd brought her up to be honest, to always tell the truth; they didn't understand where the lies had come from.

Neither did Hettie, if she were honest. But she'd explained herself the best she could, and, she thought, they were understanding enough. She was lucky to have such forgiving, kind-hearted parents, she thought. Still, she'd been glad she had work as an excuse to escape the drama of it all. It was good to have finally cleared the air, but it was still altogether too much.

Freya smiled at her on her way in. She was the only one who did. Everyone else seemed to be avoiding eye contact. Did they all already know Henry was back—and with a *wife*? News really did travel fast in small communities.

Amos was at his workbench, and Hettie bid him a good morning, as she did every day. Today, she got not reply. Her heart clenched.

*Oh no,* she thought. *Not you, too.*

She didn't press the matter, though, instead she got on with her work, avoiding the curious gazes of everyone around her. She avoided Amos, too, unable to bear it if he really wasn't talking to her.

It wasn't until after lunch that she saw him again. She had declined a break, not wanting to sit idly for any length of time today, in case her thoughts caught up with her. She went into the break room only after everyone else was gone, to make sure it was clean and tidy, ready for the next day. Except the room wasn't empty. Amos was in there, sipping a cup of tea.

"You're in here late," Hettie said.

Amos looked at her, his gaze curious. "*Jah,* I got too caught up in my work. Mr. Wright noticed and forced me to take a break, I'm afraid."

Hettie tutted. "That man," she said. "Always making us sit down and eat and drink tea. Terrible."

Amos chuckled. "Absolutely horrible," he agreed. He cast his gaze away from her, then, looking down at the table in front of him, his hand curled around the flower-patterned mug. "I heard that Henry's back. I'm sorry. You didn't deserve that."

Hettie pursed her lips and turned away from him. So, everyone *did* know. She'd thought she would have a few days before the gossip spread, but of course, that been too much to hope for. She didn't want to talk about Henry or the wedding that never would be. It didn't even help that Amos didn't appear upset about her lying. He was sad for her, and that was almost worse. She didn't want his pity.

"Thank you," she said, hearing the sadness in her voice.

She left the room, muttering about not having enough cleaning cloths. In truth, there were probably plenty at the bottom of her cleaner's tray. When she returned, the room was empty, and she breathed a sigh of relief.

# Chapter Eight

Things calmed down a little since Henry's shocking return at the beginning of the week. Hettie knew full well that people were still gossiping about her, though, and she could still see the curious and pitying look in her co-workers' eyes and in the eyes of her neighbors. And worse, her family barely looked at her at all except with disappointment and censure. They weren't unsupportive of the situation, but they still didn't fully understand why she had lied to them, and Hettie knew that her *Mamm*, at least, was quite embarrassed.

On her day off, she decided to go for a walk to clear her head. It was cooler today than it had been all week, a refreshing change as they headed into summer. Still, the sun was shining and warm, and Hettie tipped her face up to it as she walked. She spent a while by the river, watching the ducks swim past and the reeds swaying in the breeze. She let her mind drift free and found herself feeling completely calm for the first time in weeks. *Gott* had a plan for her, she was sure. She was relieved that she had asked His forgiveness and had felt His merciful pardon.

She stretched as she stood. As nice it was to spend some time in leisure, there were still chores to be done at home, and she had promised Jane she would make some savory cheese rolls for dinner.

As she was walking home, a buggy pulled up beside her. "Hettie," a familiar voice called out. "I need to speak with you."

Hettie stared up at Henry, her heart pounding rapidly, her chest constricting. She hadn't seen him since that day he'd come to the house, when everything had seemed all right between them—before he'd eloped with another woman.

"What do you want?" she demanded.

"I owe you an apology, and I want... I think we need to clear the air."

She had once loved Henry—a fact which filled her now with regret. But surely, she could give him five minutes to hear his apology. She needed it, after all, no matter how angry she was with him.

"Come. I'll drop you home too if you like."

Hettie sighed. "You're right in one thing. You *do* owe me an apology. A strong one. But I'm not going to let you take me home."

"Please, Hettie. It's a short drive. I want to apologize properly."

She shook her head and continued walking. He drove his buggy slowly, staying by her side. "Get in, please."

He looked so pathetic that she couldn't help but soften slightly.

He added, "Only to your drive. I promise. And I'll never bother you again. Never."

She sighed heavily deciding that getting in would be less of a spectacle than him following her down the road. She climbed up onto the buggy beside him. It hurt, to be this close to him —but not as much as she would have imagined. She realized with no small amount of relief that she was no longer in love with Henry Schwartz.

"Well?" she said, when Henry didn't speak. "What did you want to say to me?" Although she spoke sternly, she really *did* want to hear him out. Everything had come as such a shock. She'd never learned the reasoning behind his betrayal. Was she just not good enough, or was there more to it?

"I'm sorry," he said, his eyes dark and shadowed. "I shouldn't have left the way I did. I was... confused, blinded. I was selfish and stupid, and I'm sorry because I know I hurt you. I should have spoken to you. But you see, I didn't know what I wanted until suddenly, I did. It all became clear and I just had to leave. But I should have slowed down and thought about things, thought about you, and for that, I'm truly sorry. I hope you can forgive me one day."

"Was I really such an awful prospect?" Hettie asked, needing to know, even if his answer hurt.

He gave her a shocked look. "*Nee.* You're wonderful. But my heart always belonged to someone else. A girl I knew growing up. I had hoped to marry her then, but she chose someone else—my best friend. And then he passed away. He was always in such poor health. And I... Well, I had to see if there was still a chance. And it turned out, there was."

"So you forgot about me? Forgot we were meant to be married."

"I panicked. I was an absolute coward, and honestly, I meant to write, but I just... I didn't. I did a terrible thing to you, Hettie. I'm so, so, sorry."

Hettie watched his expression and saw his sincerity. "Thank you for the apology."

"*Can* you forgive me?"

Hettie thought of how things had been between them. There had been doubt, hadn't there? Doubt that she'd never wanted to admit. In absolute truth, she had never been completely sure of Henry Schwartz, or of their future together. And she felt now, a little, that she'd found a new direction in life—with her new job, her new friends.

*And Amos...*

She shook her head, pushing Amos from her mind. He had nothing to do with this; why was she thinking of him now?

The point was, Henry's leaving had been painful, but it had set her on a different path. And Hettie couldn't help but feel like perhaps there was a lesson there. *Gott* did have a plan for each of them. Henry was living his, and Hettie hers.

"*Jah*," she said with a sigh. "I can forgive you."

He gave an audible sigh of relief. "Thank you. That means a lot to me. I really hope you find your happiness, Hettie. You deserve someone better than me, someone who will treat you better than I did."

It was the truth, Hettie thought, and she appreciated him saying so. She decided not to ride all the way to her house with him. Instead, she got out of the buggy and walked the rest of the way. And as walked, she felt a weight slipping from her shoulders.

Perhaps now, finally, she might be able to move on.

The next day, she felt something akin to happiness. She cycled into work enjoying the fresh, spring breeze on her face. She'd had some strange dreams the night before, but she'd slept well and felt refreshed. She couldn't quite recall the trajectory of those dreams, but she was sure Amos had been there. She'd thought about him a lot that morning. She was, perhaps, more than a little fond of him. Of course, after everything, he might not want her, but she was in good spirits and couldn't help but be a little hopeful.

"*Gut* morning," she greeted Freya as she walked past the front desk. "*Gut* morning," she greeted Mr. Wright with a wave as she passed his office.

She greeted her colleagues, the few who were still in and not out on jobs.

Amos was, as usual, in the workshop. He'd been working on joinery lately, making doors and stairs and window frames— work that could be done in the shop and meant he didn't have to go onsite while he was still healing. He turned toward her as she cheerfully bade him a good morning. He frowned slightly, nodded, and turned away.

Hettie's heart fell. Were they back to this, then? Was he ignoring her? And *why*? She had hoped that at least they were becoming friends, if not anything more, but that wasn't how you treated a friend or even an acquaintance. She thought for a brief moment about asking him about it, but why should she? If he wanted to be dismissive, that was his choice.

Her good mood vanished in an instant. What was it about her that made men want to ignore her or be rude to her? Was there really something that wrong with her, after all? She pursed her lips and told herself not to be so silly. Wasn't she learning that there was nothing wrong with her? Perhaps Amos had just gotten out of bed on the wrong side. Perhaps his leg was paining him and making him grouchy. There were plenty of possible reasons for his curt behavior that didn't involve her.

So once again she threw herself into her work, focusing on getting the job done. At least she had this, she thought. Taking this job had been one of the best ideas she'd had in a while. She liked to keep busy, and cleaning for Wright Construction provided her plenty of opportunities for that.

But she couldn't quite help herself from cleaning the break room at the same time she knew Amos to be on lunch. Perhaps, she thought, he would speak to her now. But he didn't. Instead, he focused solely on his food. She said nothing to him and turned her attention to scouring the electric kettle, her heart twisting sharply in her chest.

A moment later, Amos was packing away the remains of his lunch. He stood with his crutches and left the room without so much as a single word. Hettie could have cried, but she didn't. It wasn't as though there had really been anything between her and Amos anyway, had there?

By the end of the week, Hettie was truly missing her conversations and interactions with Amos. He still hadn't spoken to her much, although she'd made the effort to be polite and bid him a good morning and good evening every day. He would barely return those pleasantries, though, and she knew others had started to notice.

"Why is Amos so cold lately?" Freya asked one day. "Isn't he feeling better now? The accident was a quite a while ago now."

Hettie was honest with her. "I truly don't know," she said. "Whatever it is, I'm not aware of it."

"Especially to you, Hattie," Freya said. "He seems out of sorts."

Hettie smiled at her, but she couldn't tell Freya about the worry swirling inside her, the thoughts that maybe she'd done something, that somehow she'd offended Amos without having realized it. Maybe it wasn't just Amos, but everyone disliked her now because of her lies, and he was just the only one who showed it.

She was embarrassed that others had noticed the friction between them. If Freya had seen it, then of course some of the men would have as well, possibly even Mr. Wright. She didn't want Mr. Wright to think she was somehow causing trouble.

This had to be resolved. She couldn't carry on like this. She would have to confront Amos. Find out if she'd done something to offend him. So that evening, when everyone else had left, she found Amos in the workshop and did just that.

"Mr. Wengerd, um... Amos, please tell me, have I done something to bother you?" she asked, her tone controlled. She was as solid as a rock, not letting her nerves shake her.

Amos looked at her, held her gaze for a moment, and then looked away. For a moment he was quiet, considering his words, perhaps, before he spoke. "You've done nothing *to me,* Mis Mast. But I think, perhaps, that I have been a fool."

"I don't understand. What do you mean?" Hettie asked. "Can you tell me what you think I have done?"

"I *saw* you, H—Miss Mast."

Hettie frowned. "Saw me doing what, exactly? What on earth are you talking about, Amos?"

"I saw you getting into Henry Scwartz's buggy last week. And I... I honestly didn't believe it. He's married now, but there you were. I was worried about you, Hettie. And then, in truth, I was upset and disappointed. I can't see how you could be taking up with him."

Hettie gaped at him. She had no words. How could he even *think* that? Anger shook her words when she spoke. "You have no idea what you're talking about. I am *not* taking up with

Henry Schwartz. He asked to speak with me, and I forgave him for eloping with another woman, which of course is really *none* of your business. I would *never* take up with a married man. How could you immediately jump to such a conclusion? You didn't even ask me, did you?"

Amos at least had the good grace to look abashed. "Hettie—"

Hettie held up a hand. "*Nee*, Amos, never mind. Just go back to not speaking to me and thinking terrible things about me. Go on."

She turned on her heel and stalked off. Dear Lord, would she ever be free of being connected with Henry in some way? And how could Amos think that of her? If he'd wondered what she was doing, why couldn't he have just asked her? Had he really so little faith in her?

She picked up the bins on her way out and threw the heavy bags into the dumpster with a loud *crash*. Then she slammed the lid Closed.

That was that, then, she decided. Whatever she'd hoped for with Amos was never going to happen. In fact, any hope she'd had for men in general was done, too. Henry, Amos, and whoever else might come along—she was done with them all.

It was time to accept the fact that she would become an old *maidel*. And that was all right with her. Better, in fact. It meant she could focus on other things. Improving her relationship with her family and her relationship with *Gott*.

There was a lot that was important in her life besides possible romantic relationships. *That* was the lesson *Gott* was trying to teach her right now, she was sure of it.

Well, she had learned that lesson now, she decided, finally and truly.

# Chapter Nine

In the ensuing days, Hettie was the one ignoring Amos. She couldn't speak to him, knowing now what he thought of her. The idea made her unhappy and slightly ill, so it was better, really, to avoid him altogether. He clearly never felt the same way about her as she had felt about him, anyway; otherwise, how could he have thought that? No, it was better to pretend he wasn't there.

She was passing through the workshop one afternoon when she heard her name mentioned. She froze and turned to see Amos standing with a couple of the other men. She couldn't help but listen, not if they were talking about her.

"Women are just like that," one of the men, an *Englischer*, said. "Up and down, moody, irrational."

One of the Amish men, a man called Abel Raab, laughed. "They don't think objective-like. They're impossible to deal with when they're angry, best to just stay out of their way."

*Ach,* were they saying she was moody and irrational? She bet Amos hadn't told them why she wasn't speaking to him, and besides, last week he had been the 'moody and irrational' one. She clenched her jaw and strode from the room.

Perhaps, she thought, it was time to move on from this place. She couldn't really continue to work here, not with Amos around every corner. When she'd started this job, it had been an escape, a way to occupy her mind and take some independence for herself. Now it felt like none of those things, and instead, she was stuck in some horrible cycle. She wanted to cry, but that was of course childish, and wouldn't help anything.

She forced herself into composure and got on with her job. That was the only thing she could do, really, until she figured things out. She avoided the break room until almost three o'clock. She was sure no one would be in there then. Even Amos had usually finished his lunch by half past two.

She pushed open the door, and her heart sank. There he was, sitting in his usual spot, eating a sandwich. He glanced up when she entered the room. For a split second, she thought she saw glad affection in his eyes, but he glanced quickly away, and she knew she was mistaken. She walked over the counter and began wiping it down as rapidly as she could. She heard movement to her side but didn't turn.

She heard something being placed in the sink and turned to look. Amos had left his cup in the sink and was walking away on his crutches, as if he couldn't get out of the room fast enough.

*This is all wrong,* she thought. People weren't meant to be at odds like this. She didn't like it. She missed Amos; missed talking to him; missed his easy smile. A smile she hadn't seen in a very long time. She knew that her stubbornness had added to the situation. *Dear Gott,* she breathed. *Help me to see my way more clearly.*

Later, as she stood in the bathroom, leaning against the sink with her eyes closed, taking deep, calming breaths, she made up her mind. She needed to leave. Not just this job. Perhaps what she needed was a completely new start. Maybe in Ohio... She had family there, after all. Perhaps, she could stay with them for a while.

Yes, she decided, this was a good idea. She needed to build something new, away from the mistakes of her past.

Ohio... she thought. Yes, maybe that could work.

Hettie thought a lot about Ohio that week. She wrote a letter to her cousin there, tentatively asking if she could perhaps come and stay for a while—maybe even permanently. She hadn't quite made up her mind, but her cousin's reply had been positive. If she wanted to leave town, now she would have somewhere to stay.

She didn't see Amos at work the next day. That was strange, but she decided it wasn't her business. Not anymore. Yet despite their misunderstandings, she was going to miss him. She already did, which was silly.

It wasn't until the evening that she found out why he wasn't there. Freya broached the subject cautiously, asking once again if Hettie had heard the news.

Hettie shook her head. She had been avoiding most of her colleagues the past few days, keeping her head down, focusing only on her work.

"He's gone and had another fall."

Hettie gasped, not quite believing what she was hearing. Another fall for Amos could be devastating.

"Is he okay?" she asked, already fretting.

Freya shrugged. "I don't know. Mr. Wright told me Amos slipped at home last night. He's in the hospital again. Honestly, I feel bad for him."

It had rained heavily the night before; Hettie had gotten

soaked cycling back from work. It was easy to see how Amos might have slipped, perhaps on his way up to the house.

Hettie sighed. "So you don't know how he is?"

"I've only heard what I told you."

Hettie had to see him. Just to make sure he was all right. That was all. She didn't even need to talk to him. Maybe there was someone at the hospital she could ask. What had happened between them didn't matter anymore—she just wanted to know how he was. *Ach,* but he must be so upset. Was he in pain? She had to go check on him.

Later, she asked Jane if she would like to accompany her to the hospital one day that week, and Jane, being the kind-hearted girl she was, agreed. It was Jane's idea this time to bring him a gift and place aside a few scones to take for him.

They set out for the hospital early a day later and arrived within visiting hours. His *aenti* was already there, and outside the ward. Hettie asked how he was.

Iris Wengerd shook her head. "He's in a bad way," she told her. "He's had surgery on his leg again. I doubt he'll ever walk without a limp, but at least they think he will walk again, so that's something. They had to wait for the swelling to subside."

"We're all praying for him," Hettie promised her. "And everyone at work is thinking about him."

She headed into the ward with Jane. In his room, Amos looked half-asleep, his face pale, dark shadows under his eyes. Hettie felt deeply sorry for him then—it hurt her to see him like this. He looked smaller, somehow, and vulnerable. The only thing she wanted to do right then was to rush to his bedside and put her arms around him, to tell him it would be all right.

*I love him*, she thought, her heart quickening. The truth caught her off guard. She had known she was fond of him, but she hadn't known the depth of it—not until that moment. How had she not realized it before?

Despite everything—all her promises to herself, her decision not to need romance, her resignation to live life alone—she had fallen for Amos Wengerd. Even if he never walked again, it didn't matter a bit. She wanted to be with him.

He turned his head toward them, tried to push himself up, and failed. He scowled in pain, and the look made Hettie wince.

"We brought you some scones, Mr. Wengerd," Jane said cheerfully, setting the basket down on the little table beside his bed. "I've heard hospital food ain't that *gut*."

"It's not bad," Amos said, his voice sounding rough.

"Would you like some water?" Hettie asked, eyeing the pitcher and empty glass on the table.

Amos' scowl only deepened. *"Nee,"* he said. Nothing in his eyes said he was pleased to see her.

*I love him, but he doesn't care for me.* The thought hurt; but then, she hadn't expected him to love her back.

"We're all missing you at work," she said.

"I thought you'd all be used to my disappearances by now." He tried to smile.

"Not at all," Hettie said. "It's an empty place without you."

He chuckled, but it was a dry, humorless sound. "What are you doing here, Hettie?" he asked then, his voice thick.

Hettie faltered. "I-I wanted to check in on you."

Amos's gaze on her didn't falter. "You don't have to."

Hettie froze. He really didn't want her here? Did he dislike her? She had thought, had *hoped*, he would be happy to see her, a friendly face. But then, they really hadn't been so friendly over the past week or two, had they?

"Very well," she said, working to maintain an even tone. She turned to her sister. "Jane, we should be going."

Jane looked from her to Amos and back again, likely wondering what on earth was going on.

Hettie turned and left the room. She would put Amos behind her now, she decided. In spite of her hopes, there was nothing between them.

"Are you all right?" Jane broached once they were outside. "You two were strange. Like you wanted to make sure it looked like you didn't like each other."

*Is that how it looked?* Hettie refused to sound upset in front of her fourteen-year-old sister and decided instead to be neutral. She should have learned her lesson after Henry, she told herself. Why did she keep falling for the wrong men?

# Chapter Ten

That evening after work, Hettie sat down and wrote to her cousin. She would take her up on her kind offer of a place to stay while she settled into her new community. She would plan to work for them on their farm, and perhaps once she was there, she would be able to find a job in town so she could support herself. After all, she had to take care of herself; she couldn't keep relying on her cousin's goodwill.

She broke the news to her family. Her parents were, as ever, supportive. It was a good idea, they said, to have a fresh new start, just as long as she made the effort to write at least once a week and to visit occasionally. It was a fairly lengthy journey, but Hettie promised she would indeed come home to see her family as often as she could.

Claire was excited for her. "What an adventure," she told her. "Oh, Hettie, you'll have such a *gut* life in Ohio. I know it."

Jane was less thrilled. Instead, tears welled in her eyes, and she sniffed loudly. "You don't have to go," she said. "You can stay here—get another job here. Why do you want to leave, Hettie?"

Her brother Michael gave a loud groan and made a face at her. Hettie hoisted him onto her lap and held him for a while, until he managed to grin again and respond to her light tickles.

It bothered Hettie to see Michael and Jane upset, but she knew it was the right thing to do. She just couldn't stay, not now, not when her mind was so filled with thoughts of Amos Wengerd.

No, she decided. Ohio would be better. Ohio was the right thing to do.

Hettie had most of her things packed. Michael sat on her bed, watching her. He had begged her not to go, initially, but Hettie felt he was finally coming to accept her decision. She had, of course, promised to write, and told him she'd visit, and that he could even visit her in Ohio. That had cheered him up —the idea of an adventure in Ohio.

Handing in her notice at work had been emotional. Mr.

Wright was sad to see her go, but Hettie knew she would be easily replaced.

Jane burst into the room and plopped down on Hettie's bed. "I can't believe you're really leaving," she muttered. "And I know why too. It's so silly, Hettie."

Hettie scowled at her. "Stop pretending like you know everything. I want to go. I *need* to go."

"*Nee*," Jane said firmly. "You don't need to go. I know you, Hettie, and I know you don't. I'm not a *boppli* anymore. I know things. You're just running away."

"I am *not* running away," Hettie snapped.

Jane sighed. "Whatever you want to tell yourself... Anyway, you go ahead and run away. But you have to do one thing for me first."

"Oh?" Hettie said. "And what's that?"

"Accompany me into town tomorrow. I want to spend some time with you before you go."

Hettie sighed. She had so much to do before she left in just a few days' time. But she couldn't deny her sister such a request, and it *would* be nice to spend some time with her. Once she left, Hettie doubted she would see Jane or any of them again for some time.

"All right," she agreed. "But only for a few hours."

Jane grinned. "*Gut.* We can even buy some ice cream if you like. You won't regret it."

Hettie *did* regret it. They were standing outside the hospital, at Jane's insistence, and Hettie suddenly realized her plan. Maybe Jane *did* know more than Hettie had thought.

"This isn't sisterly bonding time, is it?" she asked. "And where's the ice cream?"

"We can buy some later if you still want to. But there's something you have to do for me here."

Hettie scowled. Her heart was beating too fast, and she clasped her hands together to stop them from trembling. She had no desire to go in there, no desire to see Amos Wengerd, no desire to have him reject her once again.

"Come on," Jane said, and reached for her hand.

Against her will, Hettie followed Jane inside.

She didn't know why she was doing this. Perhaps she hadn't entirely let go of hope. She still somehow, foolishly, thought that things might be different. Except she *knew* they wouldn't. Amos had been quite clear. He wouldn't want her here. Jane was a romantic fool and always thought things would work out. But they didn't always work out—wasn't Henry proof of that? Well, maybe it would be a good lesson for Jane to learn, too.

They entered the ward, Hettie's heart racing and her palms sweating. She didn't want to be here.

She hung back, until Jane tugged her forward, into Amos's room.

He was sitting up, and his eyes widened when he saw her. "Hettie?" he said. He looked and sounded much better than when she had visited him the week before. "I didn't think you would come." He sounded... almost *relieved*. He gave Jane a look which made Hettie suspicious that the two of them had talked without her.

"Jane?" she questioned, looking at her sister.

"I-I'm glad you came," Amos interrupted. "I'm sorry I wasn't friendly the last time. You didn't deserve that."

*No,* Hettie thought. *I didn't.*

"Jane tells me you're moving to Ohio?"

"Oh, does she now?" Hettie glanced again at her younger sister, who at least had the good sense to look a little abashed.

Amos looked down at his hands and then back up to her. "I wish you wouldn't go."

Hettie almost laughed. "I think we both know there's nothing for me here," she told him. "I need a new start. And Ohio seems as good a place as any."

Amos sighed. He scratched at his stubbled chin. "I see," he said. His gaze flashed to Jane again.

Hettie also looked at Jane and saw her nod encouragingly at Amos. What was Jane up to?

Amos went on and she focused back on him. "If you really think there's nothing here for you, then you should go. But..." He took a deep breath. "I wish you would stay."

Hettie hardly dared to breathe. What was going on here? This was a complete switch. What had happened? What had Jane said to him?

She looked again at her sister. "What did you tell him?"

Jane grinned. "Just the truth. You like him. I didn't want you leaving. Don't be mad at me, Hettie. Okay? Don't be mad."

"You came here to the hospital without me and told him *I liked him?*" Hettie couldn't even fathom such behavior. It was impossible, simply not done. *Never* done.

"I had to tell him. You were leaving," Jane said, her voice now full of anxiety. "He asked me to bring you for another visit."

"I've been horrible to you, Hettie," Amos interrupted. "I hope you'll forgive me."

Hettie frowned. "You don't even like me..."

"Hettie Mast, of course, I like you. I haven't shown it, but... I do. That was why I was so upset when I saw you with Henry that day. I was worried sick. I feared... I feared that you, well, that you still wanted him. That I didn't have a chance."

Hettie took a step back. She could feel herself trembling and hot tears stinging her eyes.

"Are you crying?" he asked. "That's not exactly the reaction I was hoping for. Are you all right? I'm so sorry, Hettie. Sorry that I never asked you about Henry—that I assumed the worst. I do like you. *Very* much. *Ach,* are you still crying? What is it?"

Hettie shook her head, still trying to fathom what was happening. Had he just told her—*twice*—that he *liked* her?

"Hettie, please say something... Are you upset with me? I am sorry."

She took a tentative step forward to his bedside. "I'm confused... I-I'm not upset, though. Maybe, maybe I'm relieved."

Amos stared at her for a long moment, until his face broke into a smile. Hettie smiled back, and then she was laughing, both of them laughing, together.

Jane stepped forward. "Is it all right that I brought you, Hettie? You're not mad at me, are you?"

Hettie turned and put her arm around Jane. "*Nee.* I'm not mad, dear little sister. I'm grateful."

Jane giggled. "See? I told you I'm not a *boppli* anymore. I know things."

Jane grinned at her and squeezed her even more tightly. Then she let go and turned back to Amos. She saw true affection in his eyes, and her heart swelled within her.

"Will you... Will you let me court you?" he asked. "I mean, once I'm up and about again, that is."

Hettie sighed. "*Jah,*" she said. "I'd like that."

He chuckled. "Thank you. It's a bit of a drive to Ohio, but I'll make the effort."

"Hettie," Jane interrupted. "You won't go now, will you? You'll stay, won't you? Don't tell me I did all this for nothing..."

Hettie shook her head. "You didn't do it for nothing. I never really wanted to go to Ohio. I only felt I had to." Hettie had thought of it as a new start, but now she saw the truth of it. Jane, at fourteen, had seen what she didn't see—she *had* been running away—from her own heart, from Amos.

Amos was smiling; looking tired, but happy.

Hettie squeezed his hand and then let go. She turned to her sister, who was grinning from ear to ear. "*Ach,* Jane. What would I do without you?"

"Don't try to find out," Jane said, laughing.

"Never," Amos told her, laughing. "We owe you."

Hettie turned to him. "You shouldn't have told her that," she warned. "She'll hold you to it."

Hettie and Jane stayed a while longer, talking about little things—the crops, the animals, their co-workers at Wright Construction. It was good, being with him like this. Hope and anticipation blossomed in Hettie's chest. This was the fresh new beginning that Hettie needed.

She and Amos, together.

# Epilogue

*Six Months Later...*

Hettie sat on the porch, staring out at the morning sky awash with pink and gold. She still had so much to do, but she couldn't bring herself to finish any of it. Her wedding dress hung on its peg next to her bedroom door, along with the *newehockers'* dresses, all still needing adjustments.

There was baking to be done, cleaning to be handled, and preparations to make.

But Hettie's heart wasn't in it.

She and Amos were to be married in less than a week, but she couldn't help but feel as though something were wrong, as though it just wasn't going to happen. Amos had been distant lately, telling her he was busy, avoiding her. He would turn her down at the last minute, just as Henry had. She had stayed in this town for him, let herself be vulnerable again, for him. And now he was going to leave her anyway. She was going to have her heart broken all over again.

As the sun rose, she decided she couldn't let it happen. Why was she sitting here waiting for him to break it off with her? She needed to talk to him; find out if her fears were true.

She ran outside, pulled the bicycle out from the shed, and rode off, the wheels crunching over gravel. She pedaled hard, needing to be there, needing to see Amos *now*, needing to know.

She arrived at Amos's house as the sun was fully risen, just as Amos was emerging from the side door.

"Hettie," he said when she stopped the bicycle in front of him. "What are you doing here so early?" Surprise laced his words. Surprise, but no displeasure.

She just had to say it, she decided. Maybe she would sound crazy, maybe he would be angry, but she didn't care, she just needed to know.

"Are you going to leave me?" she demanded.

Amos stared at her for a moment. He went quiet, and then, "*Nee*, Hettie. I'm not going to leave you. I *love* you, and I want to marry you. Honestly, I've wanted little else for a long time now. So you have nothing to be afraid of from me."

Hettie felt a weight fall from her shoulders. He really wasn't going to leave. "I'm sorry. It's just... I haven't seen very much of you lately."

Amos smiled a little at that, although Hettie couldn't figure out why. There was nothing amusing about this.

"I'm sorry for your worry," he said, "but look, let me show you why."

She followed him then, around the back of the house and across the field toward the small orchard at the back of the property. She'd only been out here a small handful of times. Why on earth was he taking her to look at fruit trees now?

And then she saw it—the old barn that sat behind the orchard had been expanded, patched up and newly painted. The boards on the windows had been pulled down, and bright new frames and clean glass had been put it instead.

"It doesn't look like much from the outside," he said, "but let me show you."

He opened the doors and led her inside. It wasn't a dusty old barn anymore. Instead, what it looked like was a home.

Hettie gasped. She stood in a small kitchen, stone-floored with dark wood cabinets and counters. It was an open room, connecting onto the front room, sparsely decorated—just a couch, a rocking chair, and a couple of bookshelves. Still, the beginnings of a comfortable home were all there.

When on earth had Amos done all this?

"Come on," he said, and took her hand firmly in his. She followed him up a winding staircase to the open loft that looked out onto the room below. It held a large, four-poster bed a pale green dressing table, and a rag rug to keep bare feet warm in the colder months.

"It's not much," Amos said, "But I thought it could be ours. It'll give us some privacy until we can find a place of our own. As you know, there is no *daadi haus* here. I thought this would do, instead."

Hettie looked around, overwhelmed by all he had done. Had he really managed all this for her?

Amos cleared his throat, breaking Hettie from her whirlwind of thoughts. "Well?" he said. "What do you think?"

"*Ach,* Amos." Hettie said, tearful now. "I think it's wonderful *gut*. I just can't believe you did all this. And kept it a secret, too."

Amos chuckled. "Well, a few people helped me. I didn't quite manage it alone, but... it was worth it. For you. For *us*."

Hettie flung her arms around him then, holding him tightly. This was more than she ever hoped. *He* was more than she ever hoped.

"Thank you," she murmured into his neck. "Thank you, dear husband-to-be."

# Continue Reading...

Thank you for reading *The Construction Worker.* **Are you wondering what to read next?** Why not read *Amish Escape?* **Here's a peek for you:**

Marlene Burki was the last passenger to step out of the stifling heat of the overcrowded bus. She waited until all the others had pushed, shoved, and grumbled their way to the doors: a gaggle of giggling teenagers with dyed hair and glittering smartphones, a man with a briefcase barking into his phone, a harassed young mother trying to wrangle three unruly children. They were all so alien to her, and so she only moved when they had all disappeared into the sweltering summery day outside. Only then did she rise, clutching a small bag nervously in her trembling white hands, holding it close against her black apron.

The bus driver gave her a curious glance when she walked forward, his eyes raking her from her plain black *kapp* to her sturdy boots, which had no laces. Marlene was grateful that he said nothing.

Stepping out at the silent bus stop at Baker's Corner, Marlene was relieved to see that most of the other passengers had already dispersed into waiting cars. She avoided them, heading to an unoccupied bench nearby. Sitting down, she kept her bag on her lap and allowed herself a deep breath. She'd survived this leg of her journey, at least. It was almost over. And so far, it didn't seem like Jeremy had followed her.

Marlene's back ached. She wanted to lean against the bench and relax, but she found herself scanning the road up and down, taking in this sleepy little corner of a mainly Amish town. Little had changed since she'd last been here. There was still the winding main street that meandered aimlessly from one shop to another, most of them almost empty, catering to the few things that the surrounding farmers couldn't produce themselves. A horse, hitched to an open-topped buggy, was tied in front of the fabric store. Apart from the growl of the departing bus, and the ringing of hammer on steel from the smithy, there was almost no noise.

The last time Marlene had left Baker's Corner hadn't been in a bus. It had been in an open-topped buggy like that one, drawn by a fine young horse that Jeremy had just purchased. She remembered, even then, being nervous about leaving her home behind. But all she wanted was to get away from a town where everyone seemed to have a family except her. With Jeremy, she could build a new family, and she'd been trying hard to cling to that dream as she held onto his arm and waved goodbye to Aunt Sarah. The horse's hooves had sounded so cheerful then as they carried her away to the future .

She laid a hand on her belly, swallowing hard as wave of fear clutched at her. Maybe she'd been a fool to come back here. It would be the very first place he would look.

## VISIT HERE To Read More:

http://www.ticahousepublishing.com/amish-miller.html

# Thank you for Reading

If you **love Amish Romance, Click Here**

https://amish.subscribemenow.com/

to find out about all **New Hannah Miller Amish Romance Releases! We will let you know as soon as they become available!**

If you enjoyed *The Construction Worker,* would you kindly take a couple minutes to leave a positive review on Amazon? It only takes a moment, and positive reviews truly make a difference. I would be so grateful! Thank you!

**Turn the page to discover more Hannah Miller Amish Romances just for you!**

# More Amish Romance from Hannah Miller

Visit HERE for Hannah Miller's Amish Romance

https://ticahousepublishing.com/amish-miller.html

# About the Author

Hannah Miller has been writing Amish Romance for the past seven years. Long intrigued by the Amish way of life, Hannah has traveled the United States, visiting different Amish communities. She treasures her Amish friends and enjoys visiting with them. Hannah makes her home in Indiana, along with her husband, Robert. Together, they have three children and seven grandchildren. Hannah loves to ride bikes in the sunshine. And if it's warm enough for a picnic, you'll find her under the nearest tree!

Made in United States
North Haven, CT
22 June 2025

70040027R00055